# Morning Glory Monday

## Arlene Alda • Illustrated by Maryann Kovalski

Tundra Books

Published in Canada by Tundra Books,
481 University Avenue, Toronto, Ontario M5G 2E9

Published in the United States by Tundra Books of Northern New
York, P.O. Box 1030, Plattsburgh, New York 12901

Library of Congress Control Number: 2003100903

NATIONAL LIBRARY OF CANADA CATALOGUING IN PUBLICATION

Alda, Arlene, 1933-
    Morning glory monday / Arlene Alda ;
    illustrated by Maryann Kovalski.

ISBN 0-88776-620-X

I. Kovalski, Maryann  II. Title.

PZ7.A358Mo 2003      j813'.54
C2003-901132-1

We acknowledge the financial support of the Government of Canada
through the Book Publishing Industry Development Program and
that of the Government of Ontario through the Ontario Media
Development Corporation's Ontario Book Initiative. We further
acknowledge the support of the Canada Council for the Arts and the
Ontario Arts Council for our publishing program.

Design: Terri Nimmo
Printed and bound in Hong Kong, China

1 2 3 4 5 6          08 07 06 05 04 03

To Ruth Abram of the Lower East Side Tenement Museum,
whose work dignifies the everyday lives of immigrant families.

To Kathy Lowinger of Tundra Books, who knows
of the immigrant experience firsthand.

And to the Muse of Writing, whoever and wherever you are.
A. A.

For Gregory, Genevieve, and Joanna.
M. K.

That summer in the city, long ago, began the same as all the
other summers – hot, smelly, and so very noisy.

In those days, I used to play for hours and hours on our busy street
with my friend Jackie.

**G**rumpy Mrs. Grimaldi would stand outside her fish store. She never ever said, "Hello, how are you?" or "Thank you" to her customers.

Old Mr. Shapiro would work behind his big wooden barrel, slowly sorting out his pickles calling, "One for two pennies. Six for two nickels."

At night, when the streets were quieter, I would try to go to sleep in our very small, hot apartment.

Jackie lived across the alley from me. He didn't sleep alone. He slept with his five brothers, all in the very same bed.

**T**hat was the summer that Mama got homesick for Italy, way across the ocean. And there we were on the Lower East Side, in New York City, U.S.A.

**M**ama missed her sisters, she missed her old friends, and she missed all the quiet places she'd known as a girl.

**P**apa and I tried to think of how to make Mama
happy. Papa told jokes. I stood on my head.

**M**ama smiled a little, but mostly she ironed and
sewed and mopped the floor and took naps.

"**W**e need a change of scene," said Papa one day.
I thought of Coney Island, where there's a big
amusement park. "Not a bad idea," said Papa.

I won a booby prize at a booth. I had really wanted a big, pink stuffed dog. Instead, I got a small envelope, which disappointed me a lot. "What's this?" I asked.

The man who ran the booth smiled and winked at me. "They're seeds," he said. "Seeds can work magic, if you let them."

"Will they grow into flowers?" I asked Papa.

"I bet they will," he said. "Flowers will surely cheer Mama up."

THROW. 5¢
YOU NEVER KNOW

BALL 5¢
TOSS

At home, I planted the seeds. Every day
I watered them and said these words:

> Magic seeds,
> magic seeds,
> use all your power.
> Make Mama happier
> hour by hour.

The plants that might be growing in the
dark dirt made Mama curious.

Then one Monday, which was the same as every other summer
Monday, something poked its head out of the moist earth.
Could it be? Yes! The flowers had started to grow. I saw Mama's
face change. She smiled a big smile.

Every day the stems grew taller and taller and taller.
Blue morning glory buds opened. They grew quickly
on their twisty vines and wrapped themselves around
the fire escapes. They curled around the chimneys
on the rooftops.

"I love them! I love them!" Mama said. She hugged
and kissed Papa and me.

The morning glories didn't stop there.

**S**oon all the buildings, as far as you could see, had flowers on them.
The entire city was covered with sky blue morning glories.

**M**ama was so happy that she took care of the flowers for that entire summer, and even into the fall. The magic seeds had done their job – and not just for Mama.

**G**rumpy Mrs. Grimaldi thanked her customers every day.
She said "Hello" and "Thank you," even if they couldn't pay.

**O**ld Mr. Shapiro stopped selling his pickles.
He bought a brass trumpet to play for his nickels.

The five brothers who slept in Jackie's bed
moved up with him to the cool roof instead.

And guess what?

**M**y dear friend Jackie,
who I've mentioned before,

We grew up and married
and opened this store.